This book belongs to:

_____

D1222016

*This book is dedicated to my wife*
*For helping me be the best me I can be*

Thank you to **Hashem** for all that He gives me

Thank you very much to **my whole family**

Thank you to **Avi Goldberg, Dr. Mark Friedman,**
**R' Baruch Chait, Stuart Schnee** and ... **THE DIRA**

Thank you to **ArtScroll**

And, of course, **Darrell**.

 RTSCROLL® YOUTH SERIES

"IMAGINE IF..."

© *Copyright 2014 by* Mesorah Publications, Ltd.
First edition – First impression: May, 2014

Published by **MESORAH PUBLICATIONS, LTD.**
4401 Second Avenue / Brooklyn, N.Y 11232 / (718) 921-9000 / Fax: (718) 680-1875
www.artscroll.com

Distributed in Israel by **SIFRIATI / A. GITLER**
Moshav Magshimim / Israel

Distributed in Europe by **LEHMANNS**
Unit E, Viking Business Park, Rolling Mill Road / Jarrow, Tyne and Wear / England NE32 3DP

Distributed in Australia and New Zealand by **GOLDS WORLD OF JUDAICA**
3-13 William Street / Balaclava, Melbourne 3183, Victoria, Australia

Distributed in South Africa by **KOLLEL BOOKSHOP**
Northfield Centre / 17 Northfield Avenue / Glenhazel 2192 / Johannesburg, South Africa

Printed in the United States of America by Noble Book Press Corp.
Custom bound by Sefercraft, Inc. / 4401 Second Avenue / Brooklyn N.Y. 11232

ISBN-10: 1-4226-1491-3
ISBN-13: 978-1-4226-1491-4

# Imagine if...

Published by
ARTSCROLL
Mesorah Publications, ltd.

By
Rabbi Zeegel

Illustrated by
Darrell Mordecai

Take a long look, through your take-a-look eyes
How this world is amazing, from the sea to the skies.
But try and imagine and what would you say
If things weren't going their usual way?

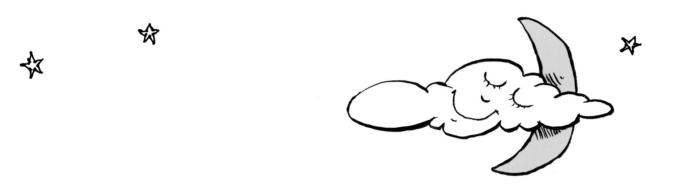

Imagine if, the night wasn't dark
Or your pet cat smiled, and started to bark.
Imagine if, for a minute or two
A cow would go naaaay and a horse would go moooo.

If the sea wasn't deep
Or an orange was red

10

Or a Lulav had sprouted right under your bed.

From knees to the bees
To the One-Legged-Furfect
Hashem has made everything, perfectly perfect.

And for who?
Why, for you!
And of course for me too.
For Moshe and Mike
And your great-great-aunt Sue.

Imagine if, people's hair would be blue
I wouldn't like it, how about you?

14

If smellicious smells came out of roses
Then people would walk, while holding their noses!

15

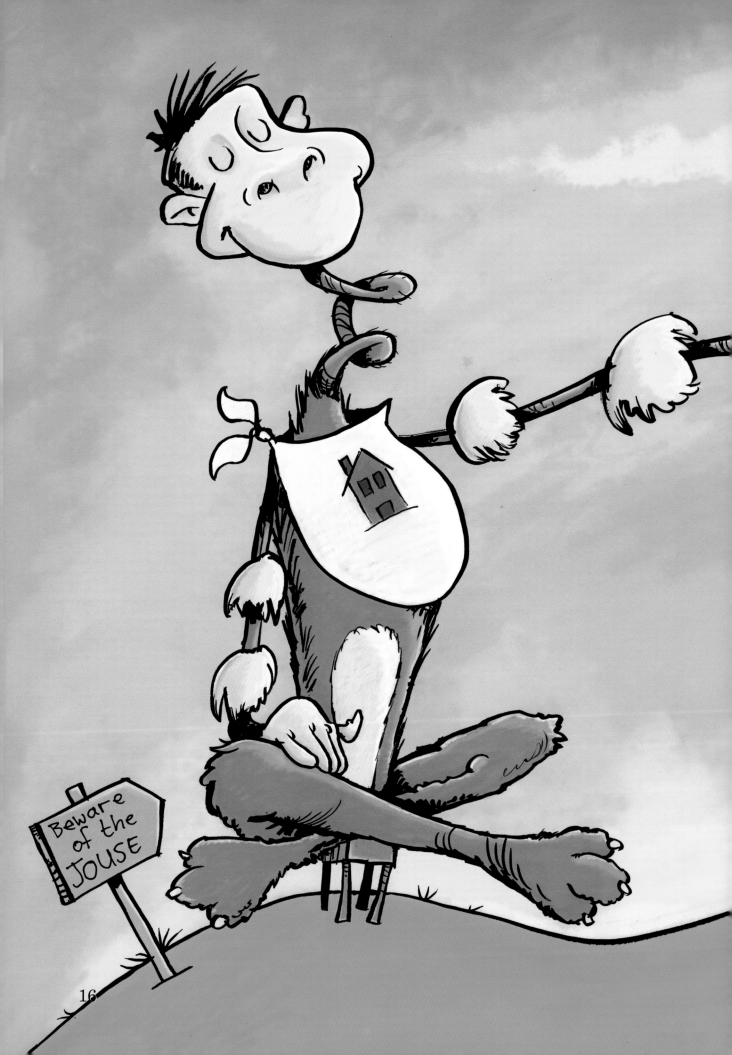

Imagine a Jouse would eat up your house
Or the house of your friend, Sir Benjy J. Crouse.

So strange and so funny, but what would you do
If Hashem had not made it, just perfect for you?

If mountains were low,
And grass was real high
And rain wouldn't rain
From up in the sky.

If the sun wouldn't set,
I'm willing to bet
A non-setting-sun
Is the strangest thing yet.

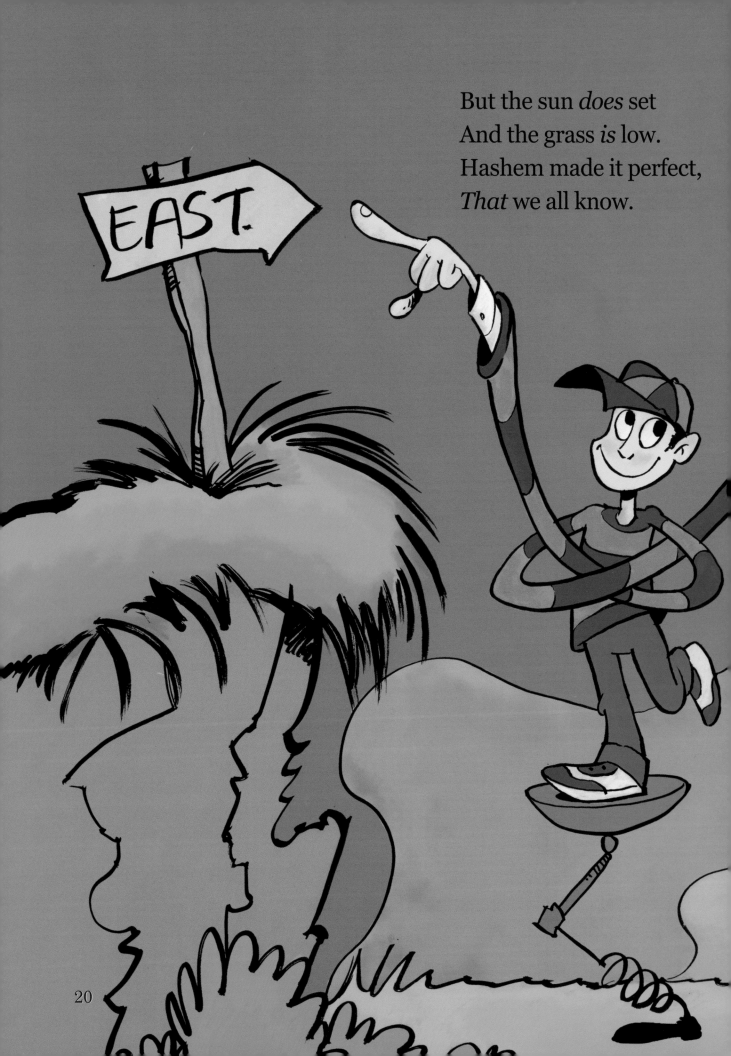

But the sun *does* set
And the grass *is* low.
Hashem made it perfect,
*That* we all know.

EAST.

From East to West
He made it the best
For Meir and Miri and all of the rest!

21

Try and imagine if snow wasn't cold
Imagine a Shofar too heavy to hold.

22

If camels would each, have six or eight humps
And trees would grow backwards, right into their stumps.

Imagine if doors, would be opened by Zoors
And what if a lion forgot that it roars.
If just apple cores were sold in the stores
*I* wouldn't shop in that core store of yours.

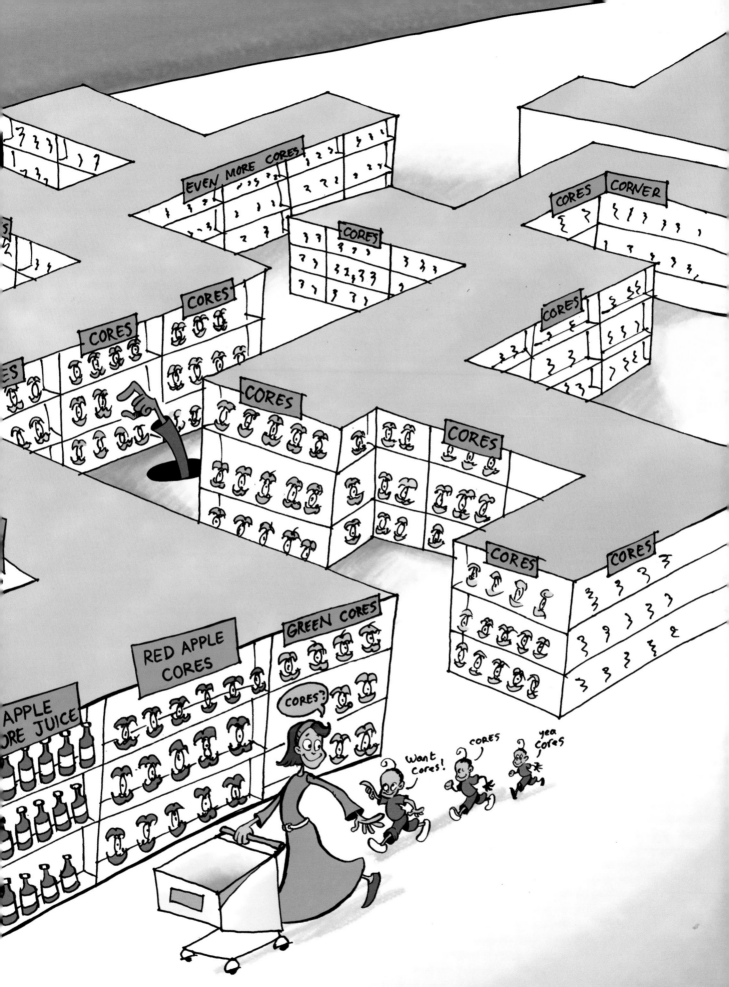

The spice and the ice
The dice, even lice!
Don't have to think twice, how everything's nice.
Hear it from me, or from Fooffer-Faff-Fice
While he eats his Fooffer-Faff fluffiest rice.

Everything's perfect, as good as can be!
For every which person, each he and each she.
When I think about *that* it makes me go yay!
This wonderful world in this wonderful way.

28

If the earth was not perfect, completely complete
Instead of your hands, you had two left feet.
If chairs would be tables, and tables were chairs
Or draidels were talking, while walking down stairs.

31

Imagine that fish never learned how to swim
Or a ball was thrown, at a hoop with no rim.
Imagine if birds never learned how to fly
What a world that would be. Who knows? Not I!

SOUTH

33

Nope, not in this world, this world's much too fine
This amazingly-wonderful-great world of mine.
You'll see some things, if you look for a while
You'll be so amazed, you'll laugh and you'll smile.

Hashem made it perfect,
We all know that's true

For him and for her,
For me...

And for you!